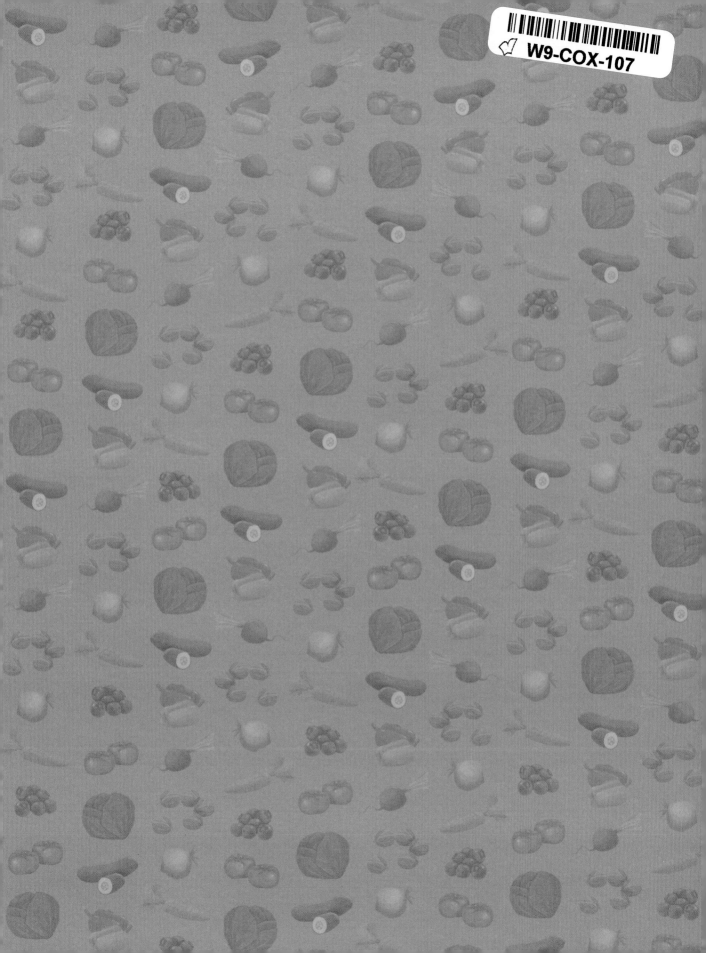

THE FOODIE FLAMINGO

by VANESSA HOWL

Illustrated by PABLO PINO

RP | KIDS
PHILADELPHIA

Running Press Kids
Hachette Book Group
1290 Avenue of the Americas
New York, NY 10104
www.runningpress.com/rpkids
@RP_Kids

Printed in China

First Edition: June 2021

Published by Running Press Kids, an imprint of Perseus Books, LLC, a subsidiary of
Hachette Book Group, Inc. The Running Press Kids name and logo is a trademark
of the Hachette Book Group.

The Hachette Speakers Bureau provides a wide range of authors for speaking events.
To find out more, go to www.hachettespeakersbureau.com or call (866) 376-6591.

The publisher is not responsible for websites (or their content) that are not owned
by the publisher.

Print book cover and interior design
by Marissa Raybuck

Library of Congress Control Number: 2019953745

ISBNs: 978-0-7624-9700-3 (hardcover), 978-0-7624-9701-0 (ebook),
978-0-7624-7317-5 (ebook), 978-0-7624-7316-8 (ebook)

APS

10 9 8 7 6 5 4 3 2 1

FOR CARMEN, MY FAVORITE FOODIE.
—VH

FOR BENJI, ULI, AND LOLA,
THE INSATIABLE FOODIES OF THE HOME.
—PP

Every Friday at the Pink Flamingo Restaurant,
Frankie Flamingo met up with her friends:
Frederick, Felicia, and Steve.
And every Friday, they each ordered the same dishes.

Frederick ordered braised shrimp.
Felicia ordered boiled shrimp.
Steve ordered buttered shrimp.
And Frankie ordered shrimp bisque.

But one Friday, Frankie learned the word *foodie*,
which means someone who thinks of every
new meal as an adventure.

So when it was her turn to order,
she asked a question.

Her friends' feathers ruffled. Steve even gasped.
"But we like shrimp," said Frederick.
"It gives us our lovely pink color," said Felicia.
"What if you try something new and hate it?" said Steve.
"It could ruin dinner!"

The server looked stern, so Frankie ordered stew
and kept her foodie feelings to herself.

The next day, Frankie went
to the market and bought
a big bag of Brussel sprouts.

She spent each night
that week blanching, boiling,

and baking the Brussels sprouts
in new ways.

Some bowls were better than others.

But trying them made her feel better, braver . . .

different than before.

Beaks turned when Frankie strutted
into The Pink Flamingo.

"Are you all right?" asked Frederick.
"You look a little green," said Felicia.
Steve just stared.
Frankie said, "I'm great," and grinned through dinner.

Each Friday dinner after that,
Frankie flustered her friends.
One week, she flew in with feathers a yeasty yellow.

The next week, she was berry blue.

Finally, after she flounced away,
purple as a plum,
her friends stayed at the table,
trying to solve the mystery.

"If shrimp turns us pink . . ." Frederick said.
"Maybe Frankie's eating something else," finished Felicia.

"But how do we know for sure?" said Steve.

Frankie's friends sneaked to her house
and spied through her window.

Sure enough, they saw her taking the tops off tomatoes
and turning them into sauce and salsa.
Then they formed a scheme of their own.

The next week, Frankie's friends got together
to try her tomato techniques.
They chopped and chilled. They steamed and sautéed.
They took turns taking tentative tastes.

It was savory and spicy. It was smooth and sweet.
Some of them liked it. Some of them didn't.
But the sauces and salsas made all of them feel like
they had flown somewhere new.

That Friday, when Frankie arrived at the restaurant,
it was her turn to be surprised.

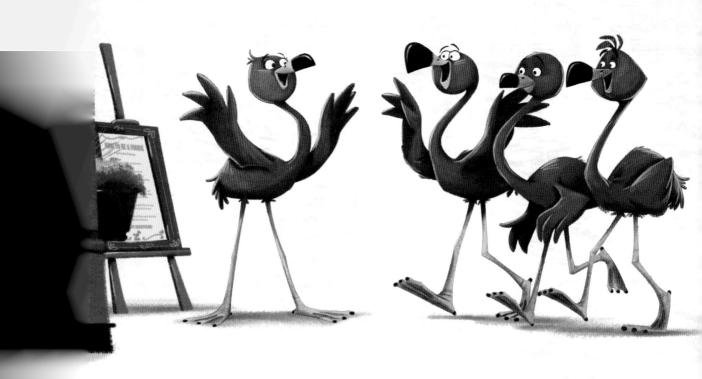

The server loved their color.
The chef asked for their secrets.
Frankie said, "We're all foodies!"

Now Frankie cooks for her friends
at the restaurant.

She is happy as a hornbill, crafting meals of every color.

Flamingos flock there for its flavors and fun,
its aromas and adventures.

It even has a new name.

HOW TO BE A FOODIE

by **Frankie Flamingo**

Try a food you've never tasted before.

. . .

Cook a meal with a friend or parent.

. . .

Take a food you already like and sprinkle something
new on top, like a spice or herb.

. . .

Close your eyes, take a sniff of your dinner, and
describe the smell in three words. Then take a bite,
and describe the taste in three words.

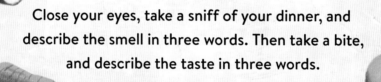

. . .

Treat your food like an art project! Place it on your
plate in a new, creative way before you eat.

. . .

Spread the word! Tell your friends about foods
that are different and delicious.

HAPPY ADVENTURING!

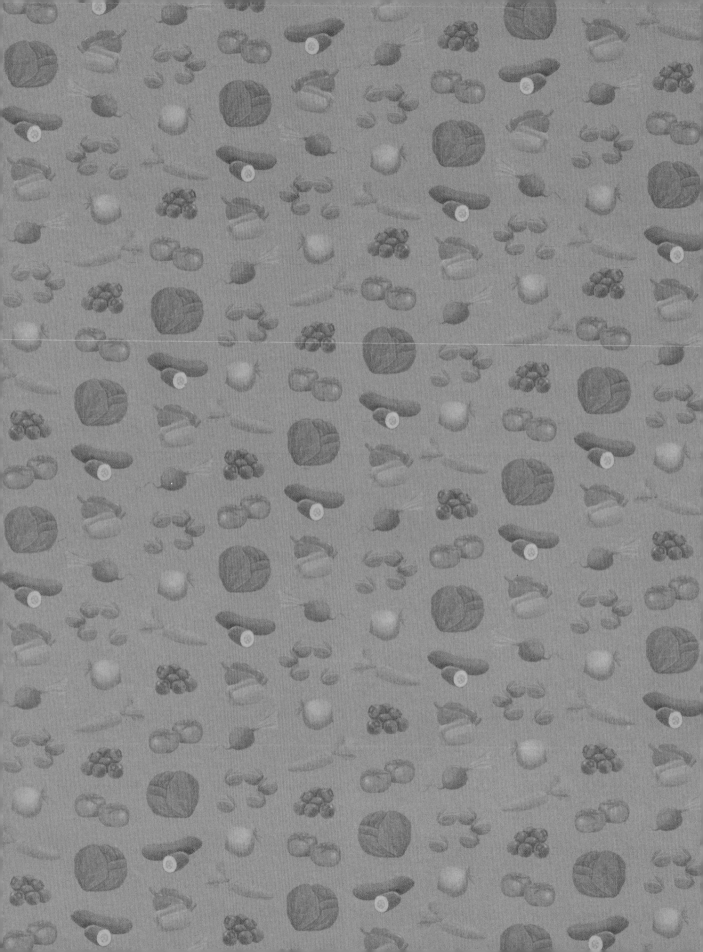